This book is dedicated to my amazing daughters, Micah, Harley, and Riley.

Although Harley is no longer with us, her incredible spirit lives on within her twin sister, Micah, and her younger sister, Riley, whom she never had the chance to meet.

www.mascotbooks.com

The Girl Who Lives in the Sky

For more information, please contact:
Mascot Books
620 Herndon Parkway #320
Herndon, VA 20170
info@mascotbooks.com

Library of Congress Control Number: 2019900013

CPSIA Code: PRT0419A
ISBN-13: 978-1-64307-349-1

Printed in the United States

THE GIRL WHO LIVES IN THE SKY

Written by
Jodi Kalson

Illustrated by
Vanessa Alexandre

There once were two girls born on the same day.

They first lived together. Then one went away.

The one who left went to live in the sky.

The one who stayed waved to her, "goodbye."

The one who stayed had a dream that night.

The things she saw were quite a sight.

She looked up and saw the girl in the sky,

eating chocolate ice cream and a whole pizza pie.

She then went to her own refrigerator,

and ate the same thing, but had a stomachache later!

She then looked up and saw the girl in a store,

shopping for toys and candy galore.

She asked her mom for toys and candy, too.

Her mom said, "Of course!" and the girl shouted, "Woohoo!"

She then looked up and saw a zoo in the sky,

and suddenly realized the elephants could fly!

But when she went to the zoo on the ground,

all of the animals were just standing around.

She then saw a party that looked really fun.

Everyone was flying around the stars and the sun.

And at the same time, it was her party, too.

She saw her cake with candles, took a deep breath, and blew.

At the end of the party, she sent balloons to the sky,

to the girl she had waved to and said, "goodbye."

And even though she knew they were now far apart,

she also knew the girl would remain in her heart.

The one who left, her
sister, her friend,

who she knew one day
she would see again.

About the Author

Jodi Kalson grew up in South Florida, graduated from the University of Florida, and received her law degree from Widener University Delaware Law School in 2007. She practiced law in Philadelphia for several years before giving birth to her twin daughters, Micah and Harley. They were born at 27 weeks in 2013. Harley was born with an extremely rare congenital defect called a type 4 laryngeal cleft and microgastria. She passed away at 8 ½ months old after spending her entire life in the Children's Hospital of Philadelphia Newborn/Infant Intensive Care Unit. Jodi was inspired to write her first book, *The Girl Who Lives in the Sky*, when Micah turned five years old and began asking where someone goes when they pass away. Jodi hopes this book will be a useful tool to help parents discuss the loss of a loved one with young children. Jodi lives in Atlanta with her husband, Richard, and their daughters, Micah and Riley.